nickelodeon

W9-CAV-911

Nella
THE PRINCESS KNIGHT

Nella's Sticker Adventure!

A GOLDEN BOOK • NEW YORK

ISBN 978-1-5247-6886-7
randomhousekids.com
Printed in the United States of America
10 9 8 7 6 5

Nella is a princess.

Nella is also a brave knight!

Draw yourself as a brave and daring knight!

Nella is not like other princesses.
Do you see the picture that is different? Circle it.

A

B

C

D

E

ANSWER: D.

Trinket is Nella's best unicorn friend.
She loves to sparkle!

Help Nella find her way to Trinket.

START

FINISH

Nella and Trinket are ready for adventure!

Sir Garrett is Nella's best friend.

Clod is Sir Garrett's trusty steed.

Which path will lead Sir Garrett to Clod?

A   B   C

ANSWER: C.

Nella is excited because there's a new flavor
at the Ice Cream Shoppe.
It's called Royalicious Plumberry.

Trinket is excited, too!

Sir Garrett and Clod wouldn't
miss this day for anything!

Ida and Uta open the Ice Cream Shoppe!

Color the ice cream purple!

Nella and Sir Garrett get the first scoops
of Royalicious Plumberry.

"Oh, no! Our ice cream—it's gone!" Nella exclaims.

"Don't look at me," says Clod.
"Even I can't eat *that* fast!"

Nella knows what happened—
some impkins took the ice cream!

Sir Garrett reads from one of his Knightly Trading Cards: "'Impkins are purple, adorably cute, and love ice cream.'"

Impkins also love to cause trouble!

"No matter how cute you are, it's not right to take other people's ice cream!" says Nella.

"After that impkin!" Nella says.

Nella transforms into a Princess Knight!

Trinket loves Nella's shiny armor.
"Dazzling," she says. "Just dazzling."

The impkin loves the ice cream and now wants a whole tub of it!

"Not so fast, little guy," Nella says as her sword changes into a bow and arrow.

Nella's arrow attaches to the tub. With a yank from Trinket, the tub flies up and away from the impkin.

"Hold on now, little fella," Nella says.

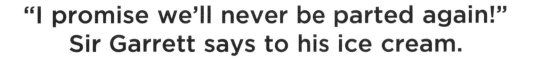
"I promise we'll never be parted again!"
Sir Garrett says to his ice cream.

Impkins are everywhere!
How many are there?

An impkin takes Sir Garrett's ice cream again!

Even King Dad's ice cream isn't safe.

"Don't worry," Nella says. "We'll get your ice cream back—and stop these impkins."

Sir Garrett and Clod join in the ice cream chase.

**Nella has an idea.
"If the impkins love ice cream so much," she says,
"why don't we just share it with them?"**

Nella gives some Magical Marshmallow Mint
ice cream to the impkins.

But the impkins don't like that flavor.
They start throwing the ice cream!

There's ice cream everywhere, and Clod loves it. Use the key to color the picture.

KEY

1 = brown
2 = black
3 = blue
4 = pink

"The only food the impkins eat is plumberries!"
says Nella. "That's why they want the
Royalicious Plumberry ice cream!"

"Those poor little guys are hungry and lost,"
says Nella. "We need to get them home.
And I know how to do it!"

Connect the dots to help Nella turn her bow into a lance.

Nella takes the last tub of Royalicious Plumberry.
She will use her lance to launch the ice cream
to the impkins.

Nella flings the ice cream.

The impkins try to catch it—
and begin to follow Nella!

Follow the ice cream! Help Nella and Trinket lead the impkins to Plumberry Hill.

START

FINISH

The friends reach Plumberry Hill.

Sir Garrett is finally about to eat his last scoop
of Royalicious Plumberry when Nella
makes a shocking discovery.

"There are no plumberries left!" says Nella.
"All of the impkins' favorite food is gone!"

With no plumberries, the impkins are sad
and even hungrier.

Getting to taste Royalicious Plumberry
doesn't seem so important to Sir Garrett now.
He gives his cone to an impkin.

"We need to think of a way to help the impkins,"
says Nella.

"There is no more ice cream," says Trinket.
"But there are plenty of plumberry seeds."

Nella wants to grow more plumberry bushes.
She flings the seeds with her lance.

The sun comes out!

Plumberries pop up everywhere!

The impkins give some berries to the ice cream makers for their Royalicious Plumberry ice cream.

The impkins share the ice cream
with Nella and her friends.

Sir Garrett and Clod finally taste the
Royalicious Plumberry ice cream. They love it!

It was a totally royalicious day!

Working together makes a difference!
Can you find five differences between the top and bottom pictures?

Follow your Knightly Heart . . .

. . . and always be EXACTLY who you are!